KIDS CAN'T STOP READING
THE CHOOSE YOUR
OWN ADVENTURE® STORIES!

"Choose Your Own Adventure is the best thing that has come along since books themselves."
—Alysha Beyer, age 11

"I didn't read much before, but now I read my Choose Your Own Adventure books almost every night."
—Chris Brogan, age 13

"I love the control I have over what happens next."
—Kosta Efstathiou, age 17

"Choose Your Own Adventure books are so much fun to read and collect—I want them all!"
—Brendan Davin, age 11

And teachers like this series, too:
"We have read and reread, worn thin, loved, loaned, bought for others, and donated to school libraries our Choose Your Own Adventure books."

CHOOSE YOUR OWN ADVENTURE®—
AND MAKE READING MORE FUN!

SECRET OF THE NINJA

BY JAY LEIBOLD

ILLUSTRATED BY S. FREYMANN

An R.A. Montgomery Book.

BANTAM BOOKS
NEW YORK · TORONTO · LONDON · SYDNEY · AUCKLAND

RL 5, IL age 10 and up

SECRET OF THE NINJA
A Bantam Book / April 1987

CHOOSE YOUR OWN ADVENTURE © *is a registered trademark of
Bantam Books. Registered in U.S. Patent and Trademark Office
and elsewhere.*

Original conception of Edward Packard.

ISBN 0-553-27565-8

Published simultaneously in the United States and Canada

---

*Bantam Books are published by Bantam Books, a division of Bantam
Doubleday Dell Publishing Group, Inc. Its trademark, consisting of the
words "Bantam Books" and the portrayal of a rooster, is Registered in
U.S. Patent and Trademark Office and in other countries. Marca Regis-
trada. Bantam Books, 666 Fifth Avenue, New York, New York 10103.*

PRINTED IN THE UNITED STATES OF AMERICA

OPM   18   17   16   15   14   13   12

WARNING!!!

Do not read this book straight through from beginning to end! You can have many different adventures as you try to find out what mysterious force is disturbing your friend Nada's martial arts school. As you read, you will be able to make choices. Your choices will determine whether you succeed in solving the mystery.

As you search for clues, you'll encounter the secret and sometimes magical world of the ninja. You may even have to become a ninja yourself. *You* are responsible for your fate because *you* make the decisions. After you make a choice, follow the instructions to find out what happens next.

Be careful! The ninja can be deadly. To find out more about them before you begin, read the Special Note on the following pages.

SPECIAL NOTE ON THE NINJA

The ancient art practiced by the ninja is called *ninjutsu*—the way of stealth or invisibility. It grew out of many sources, including Japanese fighting arts *(bujutsu)*, Chinese war tactics, Tibetan mystical practices, and Japanese mountain religions. Mountain clans developed the art and passed it secretly from one generation to the next. Because the ninja were commoners, they were not held to the samurai's rigid code of behavior, and by subtle means they could accomplish things a samurai could not. *Ninjutsu* is also a martial art that has always been practiced by both men and women.

A ninja has many different skills. Each *ryu* (tradition or school) has its own mix of techniques, taught by the *sensei* (teacher or master) at the *dojo* (the physical place where martial arts are practiced). A student might specialize in hand-to-hand fighting, swordsmanship, or the use of various other weapons. He or she might learn how to move without being detected, how to scale walls and trees, or how to deceive an enemy with special tactics. Some ninja used their art simply to defend themselves and their villages, others for espionage and commando attacks, and some even became hired assassins.

Most of the adventures in this book are drawn from Japanese folk legends and beliefs. According to legend, the ninja were first taught their art by mountain beings called *tengu,* who also taught them sorcery, or *kuji.* Mystic finger positions, trance, and hypnotism help the ninja channel energy. Most ninja use these techniques as part of a spiritual way of living, but some misuse them to manipulate others.

GLOSSARY

Aikido—*Ai*, harmony; *ki*, energy; *do*, the way. A defensive discipline using pivoting motions and the momentum of the attacker to neutralize the attack.

Biwa—A four-stringed instrument similar to a lute.

Bujutsu—Broad term for all Japanese warrior arts.

Daimyo—A feudal lord.

Dojo—The place where martial arts are practiced.

Furoshiki—A large kerchief used to tie up and carry one's belongings.

Futon—A thick, quilted mattress.

Gen—Illusion. A wise man is quoted as saying this world is *gen*, a marionette show.

Gohei—Sacred wand used by mountain priests.

Goryo Shinko—The practice of building shrines or holding festivals to pacify vengeful spirits. Based on the belief that if someone dies with resentment, his or her spirit will haunt the living.

Haragei—A kind of sixth sense, a way of being grounded within oneself and attuned to inner energy. *Hara* is one's center of gravity, a point two inches below the navel.

Jonin—Leader of a group of ninja.

Kaginawa—A grapple or hook attached to the end of a rope.

Kami—A spirit, demon, or deity.

Karate—Literally, "empty-handed." A martial art utilizing punches and kicks.

Kimono—Robelike garment, usually cotton or silk, worn by men and women.

Koto—A silk-stringed musical instrument resembling a zither.

Kuji—Ninja sorcery. Sometimes described as "nine hands cutting" or "nine syllables." Mystic finger positions channel energy.

Kusari–fundo—Ninja weapon; a length of chain with weights at either end.

Miko—A priestess or maiden in service of a shrine; also, a sorceress.

Ninja—An adept at the art of ninjutsu.

Ninjutsu—The "art of stealth" or "way of invisibility." An unconventional discipline incorporating martial arts, special weapons, techniques of concealment, and sorcery.

Rojo—House mistress, woman in charge of the domestic staff.

Ronin—Literally, "man tossed by the waves." A freelance samurai who had no master and usually no consistent employment.

Ryu—School or tradition of martial arts.

Saiminjutsu—Ninja hypnotism.

Sake—Japanese rice wine.

Sakki—A kind of sixth sense or ability to detect harmful intentions—"the force of the killer."

Samurai—Japanese feudal warrior. The samurai were the highest class, followed by farmers, craftsmen, and finally merchants. Samurai were also the administrators of the state.

Sensei—Master, teacher.

Seppuku—Ritual suicide, an honorable form of death for samurai.

Shugendo—A Japanese mountain religion incorporating ascetic practices and magic. The traditional founder of Shugendo is En no Ozunu, sometimes called En no Gyoja. Practitioners of Shugendo are called *yamabushi*.

Shuriken—A metal throwing blade, often star-shaped.

Tatarigami—Ritual trance.

Tengu—Mythical creatures supposed to have first taught ninja their art. Sometimes portrayed as helpful but mischievous, other times as devilish, *tengu* are often shown with long noses or beaks, wings attached to the body of an old man, and long claws or fingernails. They wear capes of feathers or leaves, live in trees in the mountains, and, according to one description, are the condensed spirit of the principle of *yin*, or darkness.

Tengu–bi—*Tengu* light, eerie phosphorescence that flickers between the trees in the mountains where *tengu* live.

Tengu–kaze—*Tengu* wind, a whirlwind that lifts people into the air.

Yamabushi—Literally, "one who lies down on the mountains." A Shugendo priest, ascetic, or magician.

Thunder crashes and lightning splits the sky above you with such force, it seems the sky will shatter. You run for cover. Rain pours down in sheets, pounding you like a fist. The storm seems to want to destroy everything beneath it.

Once inside the sliding doors of the *dojo,* you stand with your friend Nada, both of you soaked to the skin, and watch the storm vent its rage. Another tremendous clap of thunder shakes the building to its foundation.

Turn to page 2.

Nada casts a sidelong glance at you as if to say, "See what I mean?" The two of you sit cross-legged on the floor, unable to take your eyes from the tempest outside. "Third one this week," Nada murmurs. "And this is the dry season."

The thunder and lightning finally give way to a steady downpour. Nada stands up and says, "Let's get you some dry clothes." You follow her to a back room where she hands you a towel and a kimono.

As you dry off and change, you retrace in your mind the history of your friendship with Nada. You'd studied karate in California before spending a summer in Japan. There you met Nada and found you shared many ideas about martial arts. She introduced you to a new discipline called aikido. A year ago you moved to the city of Kyoto to pursue aikido more intensively. You and Nada became best friends. You were sad when Nada returned three months ago to her family's *dojo* in Nara, but you have kept in close touch.

Now, as you tie your kimono and prepare to join Nada for tea, you wonder why she called you so urgently to Nara this morning.

Turn to page 4.

The *sensei* looks back and forth between you and Nada. Then he places his palms on the table and says, "Nada, you come from a long line of warriors—though for many centuries they have practiced their art for peace, not war. I am old now. You must be the one to confront this danger."

Nada bows to the *sensei*.

"So," he says, leaning back from the table, "what course of action do you suggest?"

There is silence. The rain has stopped. You speak up: "Maybe we should take a look at the sword, and then try to track down the person who sent it."

The *sensei* nods. "A good plan."

"There is another option," Nada says. She hesitates before continuing, "I said the presence seemed very old. We could go back in time to find its origin."

The *sensei* glances sharply at Nada. She holds up her hand to stop him from speaking, and says to you, "I will explain later. Let's just say we should consider it a possibility."

If you think you should try to track down the donor of the sword, turn to page 78.

If you think it may be a good idea to go back in time, turn to page 17.

4

"'Strange things have been happening here,'" Nada says, pouring hot water over the crushed leaves in the tea cups. "The storms are just one sign that something is wrong. There have been others." With a reed whisk she stirs the leaves into a green froth in each cup, then gives you one. You hold it in both hands, letting the warmth seep in. "But even without the signs, I can sense a presence here that is new—yet at the same time ancient."

You savor the bitter taste of the tea and look across the low table at Nada. "Maybe you should start from the beginning."

Nada shifts her weight on the reed mat. "About a month ago I started noticing things disappearing and reappearing in odd places. Then there were weird noises, shrieks, laughter. Now this week, the thunder. By themselves, these do not prove anything. It is *sakki* which tells me there is a very powerful force here that wants to destroy us."

"Sakki?"

"A kind of sixth sense I learned in my training many years ago. I can feel the presence of harmful intentions."

"Did anything else happen around the time these signs appeared? Any new arrivals or changes in the *dojo*?"

Go on to the next page.

"No. . . . Wait, yes, there was a new arrival—but not a student. It was a sword. An anonymous donor sent it to us, saying it was fitting that we should have it. We didn't know what to make of it."

"Was there anything unusual about it?" you ask.

"To tell the truth, I didn't pay much attention. As you know, I'm not a big fan of weapons, although I have to admit it was beautiful. I do recall some odd markings on the hilt."

"Have you talked to the *sensei* yet?"

"A little. He refuses to believe we are threatened. But now that you are here, I will ask him to join us."

Turn to page 8.

A split-second after you grab Nada's arm and dive into the woods, a wall of flame erupts on the road, and a net lands over the spot where you were. From nowhere appear five ninja, armed with all manner of swords, staffs, and blades.

Nada pieces together a bow from her *furoshiki* and disables two of the ninja with arrows before the others detect your position in the bushes. They split up, two going to the right and one to the left.

Nada tilts her head to the right, indicating she'll take those two. You nod, and she disappears.

You find a depression in the forest floor and burrow down into it. You cover yourself with leaves and twigs, then wait for the other ninja.

The foot is next to your face almost before you know it. You grab it and push it out from under the ninja, sending him to the ground. You sit up and pivot to pin him, but he springs to his feet and draws his sword. With shock you realize that it is the sword from Nada's *dojo*!

You meet his attack with aikido defense, grabbing the ninja's sword arm with your left hand. You bring it down to your right hand, across your left leg and up and over your right shoulder. The sword flies off to your right, and your attacker hits the ground.

For a moment you hesitate between getting the sword while it's loose and preventing the ninja from rising again.

If you go for the sword, turn to page 18.

If you go for the the ninja, turn to page 108.

The *sensei* is a slight man with a few wisps of white hair on his head and chin. He bows as Nada introduces you, then sits at the tea table, back straight, waiting for Nada to speak.

"Surely you are aware of what has been occurring at our *dojo* lately," she begins.

"Yes," he replies in an even tone. "But we've discussed this. In my opinion, it will pass if we remain calm."

"Didn't you hear the thunder today?" Nada insists impatiently.

"It is true that in the old days such a storm was taken as a sign of war. But . . ." He shrugs.

Nada stands up. "*Sensei*, we must do something! A presence here wants to destroy us!"

The *sensei* looks at you. "Surely Nada's mother could see into the future when she named her child. Do you know what 'Nada' means?"

"Doesn't it mean the rough, open part of the sea where navigation is difficult?" you ask.

"Exactly," the *sensei* responds, smiling. "But someday, perhaps when she becomes *sensei* herself, she will learn patience."

Turn to page 14.

The next thing you are aware of is opening your eyes and finding yourself standing beside Nada in a rice paddy. Steep wooded hills rise on either side of you.

"Let's go," Nada says.

"How do we know where to go?"

"We don't," Nada replies, wading to an embankment.

"What do you mean?" you ask.

"How can we know where to go? We must let ourselves wander, and sooner or later we'll find what we need."

"But don't you have a plan?" you insist.

"Yes," she says, "my plan is to wander aimlessly until we find something or someone who looks like they know something."

Reluctantly you follow Nada up the embankment to a road running along the edge of the valley. Until now Nada has seemed to know exactly what to do next. You begin to wonder what you've gotten yourself into.

Where the paddy stops, the valley narrows. All is quiet except for the trickling water of a creek. You're approaching a bend in the road when some wild geese in a pond take off in startled flight. You wonder what frightened them. Suddenly you want to dive away from the road.

If you grab Nada and dive into the woods, turn to page 6.

If you decide you are getting too jumpy, turn to page 82.

Sanchiro brings the sword down. It strikes your neck, and the tip breaks off. He looks at the broken blade in disbelief, then looks at you and slowly realizes what has happened. Suddenly he looks very scared. He drops the sword and flees into the woods.

You turn to Nada and say, "I guess we showed him."

Nada nods. "Let's go back to the *dojo*."

The End

"My training included *kuji*," Nada continues. "It's a kind of sorcery that calls up certain forces of the universe. Once you begin to tap into these forces, the stuff the present moment is composed of—matter and time—starts to seem very fragile and also quite changeable. It's like learning to open a door you didn't even know existed."

"You would have to understand the principle of *gen*," the *sensei* says.

"*Gen* means illusion," Nada explains. "Think of the physical world, including our bodies, as a conglomeration that can and will be dissolved. There are ways to slip between the cracks, if you can find the right vibration of matter and time. I know this is a very general description, but to go into any more detail would literally take years."

"There's only one problem with your plan, Nada," the *sensei* says. "It's too dangerous. You have not practiced *kuji* for years, and you know how risky it is to go into the past."

"But it's our best hope," Nada protests. "With your help, I think we could pull it off."

"At least we could try to find out more about this *kami,* if that's what it is, before you risk such a thing," the *sensei* says.

"How?" you ask.

Go on to the next page.

"*Tatarigami,*" he replies. "Trance."

"But you or I could never be the vehicle," Nada says to the *sensei.*

"That's true," the *sensei* says. He looks at you.

"It's like being hypnotized," Nada explains to you. "The *kami* is invited to speak through you and let its wants be known. But it is just as dangerous as going into the past, if not more. The *kami* may possess you."

"But we would have Tatsumo, the Shugendo priest, conduct the trance," the *sensei* counters.

"Still, if it's an especially powerful *kami* . . ." Nada's voice trails off.

If you decide to agree to be put into the trance, turn to page 54.

If you would rather not, and want to go straight into the past, turn to page 40.

Your attention is distracted by several greenish lights, the size of fists, flickering above the cypresses outside. "What are those?" you ask.

As Nada and the *sensei* turn to look, a bolt of lightning comes from nowhere and strikes the tallest tree, splitting it in two. You cringe at the thunderclap that immediately follows. Then there is silence.

The *sensei* looks stunned. Nada is bristling. "Now are you convinced?" she demands. "What more do we need? That was our sacred tree. We must defend ourselves."

The *sensei* bows his head. "Nada, you are right. I did not think such things were possible in these days—thunder and lightning attacking us! You would think we were back in the days of our ancestors."

"Perhaps," Nada says, "the days of our ancestors have come forward to us."

"What do you mean, Nada?" the *sensei* asks.

"As I was telling my friend, I feel an ancient presence here. *Sakki* tells me it is hostile. I don't know how else to explain it. It may be a *kami*."

"What's a *kami*?" you ask.

"It's similar to a spirit," Nada says. "Spirit never dies, only circulates. Everyone and everything has a spirit, and the spirit can filter through the world around us. If a *kami* is bothering us, it's our job to find out what it wants."

Turn to page 3.

You follow a road that climbs slowly toward the mountains.

In the afternoon you reach a mountain village of thatched houses shrouded in dense evergreen trees. A hush hangs over the village.

"Everyone's probably working in the fields," Nada whispers.

Finally you meet up with an old man who directs you to a trail that leads up the mountain to the house of the Mikiaka sisters, who are *miko*. As you climb you ask Nada what a *miko* is.

"Some *miko* are priestesses who tend shrines," she answers. "Others are sorceresses. Some are even ninja."

The trail ends at a sagging little cottage perched on the mountainside. You knock twice on the door. It is opened by a bent woman with iron-gray hair. "What do you want?" she demands.

"Pardon, honorable *miko,* we are hoping you can answer a question for us," Nada says.

"Don't stand in the doorway, sister, let them in," you hear a voice say from inside.

Grumbling, the woman at the door moves aside and allows you to enter. A tall, straight-backed woman with pure white hair greets you. "Sit down, honored guests, and have a cup of tea. My name is Yukio, and this is my sister, Gin."

"We are honored," Nada says, bowing and introducing herself and you.

You show the women the markings on the sword. "We understand you are *miko,*" you say. "Can you tell us where this comes from?"

Turn to page 27.

"How can we go into the past?" you ask.

"Well," Nada says, "first I must tell you something. Do you remember when we first met, one of the things that brought us together was our interest in moving beyond aggressive forms of *bujutsu*, martial arts, in favor of aikido? We talked about how aikido provided a way to integrate our physical, mental, and spiritual energies, and how it drew on inner balance to give us not only a means of self-defense, but also a way to live. In your case, it was karate that you left behind."

"And you too," you put in.

"That's not entirely true. You see, my family has for many centuries been a ninja clan. I was trained in *ninjutsu*."

It takes a moment for this to sink in. Then you ask, "Why did you stop?"

"One never really stops," Nada replies. "I just wanted to focus on aikido. But I did put away my tools of *ninjutsu*. I was afraid of what was happening—afraid I was on a violent path. It's the old problem: if you invest too much time in learning the techniques of death, you tend to want to use them. Perhaps some day, when I am wiser, I will resume my training."

You nod, absorbing this information. You'd heard amazing stories about the ninja from your mother. In addition to *bujutsu*, ninja were supposed to be skilled at stealth, invisibility, and even magic. You'd always been curious to learn more about *ninjutsu*—and now it turns out your best friend is a ninja!

Turn to page 12.

You retrieve the sword and face the ninja. He is on the ground, staring at you. You feel you're looking into two lifeless, bottomless wells. You try to look away, but can't. Nada makes her attack on the other two ninja, but you are frozen.

The ninja yells a code word, causing the other two to duck away from Nada and retreat to their injured comrades on the road. Helplessly you watch as he then takes the sword from your hand and escapes with his accomplices.

Nada immediately sees your condition when she comes to check on you. She twists her fingers in a series of *kuji* signs, and slowly your nervous system recovers.

"Don't let them get away!" you gasp. "They have the sword—the same sword that was sent to the *dojo!*"

Nada rushes after them, but soon returns. "They've disappeared," she says.

You and Nada find a place in the woods to camp and to recuperate from the fight. Over a dinner of rice and vegetables you discuss what happened.

"We must have just stumbled into an attack that was meant for someone else," you say.

"Yes," Nada agrees, "or they wouldn't have left without finishing the job."

"At least we know who has the sword," you say. "I guess all we can do tomorrow is try to find where they came from."

Go on to the next page.

In the morning you set off down the road. Like most roads in feudal Japan, the one running through the valley is narrow, made mainly for horse and foot travel.

After a few miles you come into a larger valley. You wade across a wide, shallow river. On the other side, the road ends at an intersection. To your left, mountains rise in the distance, and to your right, the valley widens.

You and Nada stand at the branching paths. "I don't know which direction is better," Nada says. "You choose."

If you turn left, toward the mountains, turn to page 16.

If you turn right, into the valley, turn to page 31.

"Maybe the *tengu* can help us," you say.

"Oh, they can help," Gin assures you. "The question is *will* they? They're as likely to eat you."

Gin takes you outside and points to a mountain across the way. "I know *tengu* live up there. One named Xenglu is particularly knowledgeable. I'll show you a secret path that will lead you to a bridge across the ravine between the mountains. Watch for *tengu-bi*—the lights of the *tengu* flickering on the mountaintop."

You thank Gin and Yukio and head down the secret path with Nada. You come to the bridge, a flimsy rope and plank rigged across the deep ravine.

"We'd better go one at a time," you say.

You cross first. You must hold on to the ropes with both hands to keep your balance. After you reach the other side, Nada starts across.

A winged shadow passes over you. You look up to see what looks like an enormous bird circling above. As it swoops down on Nada, you're shocked to see that it has a wrinkled red face, a long nose, and a human body. It's a *tengu*!

The *tengu* sinks his claws into Nada's back and starts pulling her away. Nada clings desperately to the ropes of the bridge, yelling curses at the *tengu*. Should you attempt to pry the *tengu*'s claws loose? Or should you try to knock it out with a *shuriken*— a metal throwing blade?

*If you want to try to free Nada,
turn to page 23.*

If you reach for a shuriken, turn to page 103.

22

You follow Nada through the secret door. You find yourselves in a long, narrow passageway. You silently feel your way through the darkness. You listen closely for sounds ahead of you.

You come to an intersection where you feel out passageways going in four directions. A small sound to your right draws you that way. You follow the passage until suddenly it ends. You feel along the walls.

"I've found something," Nada whispers after a minute. "It's just within my reach. I think it's the bottom rung of a rope ladder." She reaches up, grabs the rung, and starts to pull herself up.

"Wait!" you say. "Don't you think there's something strange about this?"

"What do you mean?" Nada asks.

"There are always just enough clues to keep us on the trail. It's as if whatever is in front of us *wants* us to keep following. I feel like we're being lured. I think maybe it's tracking *us*, not the other way around."

"You might be right," Nada says. "But we're so close to it now, I don't want to lose it."

"I'll bet it's waiting for us at the top," you argue. "It'll have us just where it wants us, and we won't be able to escape."

"True," Nada says, "but we have the advantage of knowing it's a trap. We can devise a strategy."

If you agree to go ahead and climb the ladder, turn to page 96.

If you tell Nada you want to try a different way, turn to page 100.

You run onto the bridge and start prying the *tengu*'s claws from Nada's back. The *tengu* just laughs and knocks you away with a wing, then flies off with Nada. You have to grab for the ropes on the bridge to keep yourself from falling.

You manage to pull yourself back onto the bridge and get to safe ground. Your only thought is to find Nada and rescue her from the *tengu*. Already darkness is setting in.

You take off up the path. The light slowly drains from the world around you, and soon you are feeling your way among murky shapes along the path.

Rumbling comes from the mountaintop. In glimpses between tree branches, you catch sight of a strange bluish light flickering among the trees high above you on the ridge to your right. *Tengu-bi*, you think.

You pick up your pace, but suddenly your attention is caught by a sound in the woods. It seems incredible, but what you hear is a *koto*—a silk-stringed instrument like a zither. You've never heard music so eerily beautiful. It seems to trickle from the stars and trees. You wonder if whoever is playing might be able to help you with the *tengu*.

If you go toward the koto *music, hoping it might lead you to the* tengu, *go on to the next page.*

If you keep going after the tengu-bi, *turn to page 110.*

Pushing aside branches and bushes, you make your way through the woods toward the music. When you get closer you see firelight playing on the treetops ahead of you. You come to the edge of a clearing, where you find an astounding scene: a ring of *yamabushi* with sparkling eyes are dancing in the firelight, drinking sake, and feasting on fish and rice.

One of the *yamabushi* sees you and motions for you to join in. You begin to say, "I just want to ask a question—"

"There is time for questions later," he interrupts, pulling you into the circle. "Now is the time to dance. Come dance for us."

The music stops and then a new, slower song begins. "Dance!" the *yamabushi* cry eagerly.

If you decide to dance, turn to page 95.

If you would rather leave quickly, turn to page 114.

"I'm glad you enjoyed yourself with my friends last night," the *tengu* says, a sparkle in his eyes. "We especially enjoyed your dance!"

"We were there in the form of *yamabushi*," Nada explains. "It was an excellent performance—which is lucky for me, because if you hadn't joined in, I would have been stuck here as Xenglu's servant for the rest of my life."

"A pity too," Xenglu says. "We've been getting along so well. Nada has told me all about the ninja you fought with—a man who, I'm sorry to say, learned his powers from me."

"The ninja's name is Sanchiro Miyamotori," Nada says. "My family and the Miyamotori were enemies for a long time. According to Xenglu, Sanchiro's *kami* has been harassing our *dojo*. He put a curse on our family."

"I gave him his sword," Xenglu explains. "Once we take away its power, the curse will be lifted. Here's what you must do. You and Nada will meet up with Sanchiro on a country road. You'll be dressed as farmers. Sanchiro will demand that you move out of his way. Do not move—let him strike you."

"It is time for us to go," Nada says. She turns to Xenglu. "I'm glad we met, but I'm also glad I'm leaving. Good-bye."

Turn to page 30.

"The markings are an ideogram of some kind. Wherever it came from, it's evil," Gin says.

"We think it belongs to a ninja clan or *ryu*," Nada explains.

"It does resemble the crest of the Miyamotori," Yukio says. "But I'm afraid we can't help you more than that. I'll tell you what you should do. A wise old *yamabushi* named Gyoja lives higher up on the mountain. I'm sure he could tell you—"

"No, no," Gin interrupts. "If it's ninja you want to know about, you must seek out the *tengu* on the mountain across the ravine. The ninja first learned their art from *tengu*."

"That's a terrible idea," Yukio objects. "You should avoid the *tengu*. They like to play tricks, and their tricks are not funny."

"What's a *tengu*?" you whisper to Nada. "And what's a *yamabushi*?"

"A *yamabushi* is a mountain priest," Nada explains quickly. "A *tengu* is a creature that's supposed to look like an old man with a long beak and wings and know strong magic."

"*Tengu* are very ornery!" Yukio breaks in. "They set fire to houses, eat babies, and deceive Buddhist monks. I would go to Gyoja."

"*Tengu* can be mischievous," Gin admits, "but they know more about ninja than any monk, and they *have* been known to help people."

If you decide to look for the tengu, *turn to page 20.*

If you decide to try to find Gyoja, turn to page 44.

"I guess I'm outvoted," Nada replies with resignation.

You take off down the road, led by the samurai, who tells you his name is Sashami. You follow him through the abandoned village, and finally end up on a larger road that appears to be a main thoroughfare.

We'll be safe here," Sashami says. "The Yakuzi stay away from highways like this."

As you walk down the road with Sashami, a cry comes from behind, "Down! Down!"

A procession is approaching. Sashami and Nada immediately prostrate themselves on the side of the road, and you do the same.

You peek as the horseback samurai pass with their porters and servants. In the middle of the procession is a palanquin carried by two men, containing the *daimyo,* or lord. The procession stops, and two samurai approach. "The *daimyo* wants to see you," they say.

Turn to page 58.

"Good-bye," Xenglu says sadly. He flaps his wings and another whirlwind kicks up around you, lifting you and Nada off the mountain and out over the range. "It's a *tengu-kaze*," Nada explains. "A *tengu* wind."

The *tengu-kaze* deposits you, now dressed in farmer's clothes, on the road in the broad valley below. "Look out, stupid farmers!" a voice barks from behind.

You turn slowly to face Sanchiro Miyamotori, who is dressed in ninja armor. "I said get out of the way!" he bellows.

Still you don't move. He draws his sword. Suddenly you have a fear that this might be Xenglu's last trick—to set you up for Sanchiro.

If you decide to grab Nada and dive out of the way, turn to page 73.

If you stand your ground, turn to page 10.

No one in the villages along the way seems to know anything about the ninja. Then you come to a drab, unhappy little hillside village. The people look frightened when you ask about the sword. "Talk to Hitoshi," they say.

By afternoon you find Hitoshi, a thin young man with darting eyes. You describe the ninja who attacked you and Nada and ask Hitoshi if he's seen them.

"You have found them," Hitoshi replies. He gestures to a valley above the village. "They live in a castle up there. But you could never reach it by yourselves. I can take you—if you pay."

You're about to protest that you have nothing to pay with when Nada says, "We'll pay you, but not until we see the castle for ourselves."

Hitoshi considers this, then nods. "We must wait until dark," he says. He takes you and Nada to a secluded spot hidden by cedar trees. "Stay here until I come for you at dark."

After Hitoshi is gone, you turn to Nada and say, "I don't trust him. Do you?"

"Not very much," she concedes. "But I don't know what else we can do."

"He pointed to where the castle is," you say. "Maybe we could find it ourselves."

"I doubt it," Nada replies. "I'm sure there are many trick paths and traps. It's not easy to track down a ninja."

If you say you should try to find the castle yourselves anyway, turn to page 47.

If you decide it's a good idea to wait for Hitoshi, turn to page 50.

You walk up to the well slowly, watching for anything unusual. It seems safe, so, firmly gripping the stone ledge, you lean over and look down inside.

You are surprised by what you see—no ghoulish faces, just a young woman at a dressing table combing her long black hair. There is something mesmerizing about the motion of her comb. She looks up and smiles. Shock grips your heart. Unable to take your eyes off her, you're drawn into the well. Your sense of balance is gone. You drop over the edge and plunge into the cold water.

You come to the surface gasping for breath and struggling to stay afloat. Luckily, your ninja climbing tools are at your waist. There's a rope and bamboo ladder with metal claws along its length. You find a crevice in the mortar of the well wall, insert a claw, and begin to climb out.

You are about halfway up when a voice from the water says, "Wait, don't leave yet. Please rescue me from this well."

You look down. Under the water you can see an old crusty mirror. But you're already tired from your climb, and you wonder if this is another trick of the ghost of the well.

If you decide to go back for the mirror, turn to page 41.

If you decide to keep climbing, turn to page 48.

34

You pick up Nada and carry her toward the village. An old woman going by asks, "What happened to your friend?"

You hesitate for a moment, wondering if you should trust her, then say, "She's hurt. A sword wound. Do you know someone who can help her?"

"I can," the woman says. "Come with me."

You follow her to a little hut hidden away from the road. She tells you that her name is Nikkya, and she is a widow. In the hut she arranges a place for Nada, then pushes you away, saying, "Let me look at the wound."

After she inspects it she announces, "The cut is bad, but I think I can treat it. She'll have to stay here for several days. I will get the necessary things."

While Nikkya is gone, Nada whispers to you, still in pain, "There is only one hope for us. I can give you some of my powers. You must go to the castle and try to find out who the sword belongs to and what is causing the attack on the *dojo*. But you must go right away—you will only have my powers for a short while."

You nod. Using the last of her strength, Nada fixes you with her eyes and hypnotizes you. After she snaps you out of it, she says before passing out, "Go quickly. Do not worry about me. Nikkya will help me."

Turn to page 38.

You summon your last bit of strength and pull your hands apart, shaking off the trance. The *gohei* drops, and everything goes dark.

When you open your eyes, you are surprised to find yourself smashed into a corner of the room, Nada and the *sensei* straining to pin your limbs to the ground, Tatsumo pounding you on the back. When they see you have snapped the trance, they relax their hold. You are drenched with sweat.

"Do not get up," Tatsumo says, pushing you back to the floor. "Lie still." He begins to massage your legs, and the *sensei* your arms.

"How did you manage to break out of it?" Nada asks.

"I don't know," you say. "I just realized I had to before it was too late."

"It's a good thing," she replies.

"Yes," Tatsumo adds, "you were in the grip of a very powerful *kami*. You were lucky to escape it."

"What did we find out?" you ask.

"Enough to convince me we must go into the past to track down the origin of the *kami*," Nada says. "Apparently you were possessed by the *kami* of a warrior who lived long ago. As far as we can tell, he was enemies with an ancestor of mine, and is trying to fulfill a curse against my family."

"So we must go into the past to find out what the curse is and try to pacify it," you say.

"Exactly," the *sensei* agrees. "But first, you will have to train for a few days. Not only must you learn the manners and customs of the past, you must learn some basic *ninjutsu* techniques, which you may need to confront this warrior."

Turn to page 66.

Soon you hear Sanchiro take his place on the platform at the head of the chamber. "The spy has arrived?" he says. "Excellent. Send him in." A minute later Sanchiro says, "So, what news do you bring from the Kurayama?"

You listen closely. "Very important news," the spy tells Sanchiro. "Dana Kurayama is on his way to fight you. He says he can no longer allow you to terrorize the countryside."

Sanchiro laughs. "Good for him! I am glad my old enemy comes to face me. With my sword, I have no reason to fear him."

"He is not far from here," the spy goes on. "We think he'll arrive tomorrow morning."

"Very good," Sanchiro says. "But I will not wait around for him. In the morning I will meet him. And wherever we meet, we will do battle."

You continue to listen, but nothing more about the sword or Dana Kurayama is mentioned. Sanchiro dismisses the spy and his other lieutenants. Only you and the hypnotized guards remain, hidden in the side room. You try to decide what to do. Tomorrow's confrontation between Sanchiro and Nada's ancestor Dana may provide the key to the mystery. But you wonder if you should wait that long. Maybe you should confront Sanchiro yourself, now, while he is alone.

If you open the sliding doors and confront Sanchiro, turn to page 71.

If you decide to follow him tomorrow when he goes to meet Dana Kurayama, turn to page 42.

You have no idea how you know this sword move—the spinning sword draw—although you realize that the *kami* is the one who's actually making it, not you. You drop down, spin to your rear, and whip the blade in a horizontal arc. Nada sinks to the floor, and you fall backward.

Suddenly all the strength leaves your body, like a torrent flowing out of you. The knowledge you had just a moment ago is gone.

With horror you finally understand what has happened. The *kami* is leaving your body, victorious. Nada is dead. And you will soon have a murder charge to face.

The End

You run out into the night, back to the place under the cedars. You choose the *ninjutsu* tools you think you'll need, then return to the valley Hitoshi pointed out.

Suddenly the castle looms ahead. You can't believe you've reached it so quickly. You go around to the back of the castle and strap your iron climbing claws to your hands and feet. The long climb up the castle wall puts you inside the compound, but you must still get to the main tower of the castle. You move through the outer courtyards with phantom steps, hiding in the shadows.

When you reach the inner court you throw a *kaginawa*—a rope with a grapple at the end—up to a window. The grapple catches on the window ledge, and you climb up. Just below you stop and listen for sounds from inside. There are none, so you climb up and through the window.

Inside, you wait for several minutes, listening intently to the background noises of the castle.

When you're satisfied that no one is near, you begin searching the room. You can't believe your luck. The room is full of ninja battle gear, including the sword!

Your first impulse is to escape with the sword while you can. But then you wonder if you shouldn't stay and spy instead, in order to get to the bottom of the mystery.

---

*If you take the sword and leave,
turn to page 113.*

If you decide to stay and spy, turn to page 49.

40

"I think we should go into the past," you say. "But how can I come with you?"

"Saiminjutsu," the *sensei* answers. "Similar to what you would call hypnotism, only much more powerful. It will enable you to accompany Nada."

You have one more question. "How will we know what time and place to go to?"

"The markings on the sword may help us out," Nada replies. "We'll copy them down to take with us. But it's not like setting a clock. Mainly, the energy vibrating from the *kami*'s presence and the sword will direct us."

"Before you go," the *sensei* says, "you will have to do some preparation. You'll have to learn some of the basic techniques of *ninjutsu*. You will also need to learn the customs and manners of the past so that you will not seem too much a stranger."

The next week is spent preparing to set out on your search into the past. During the day you train in *ninjutsu* with Nada and the *sensei,* and at night you study Japanese history. The *sensei* rummages up some clothes that will enable you to pass for carpenters, which will give you an excuse to be traveling, since farmers were not supposed to leave their land. He also provides each of you with a *furoshiki* which you use to carry your gear.

Finally the day arrives. Nada sits you down on a bench in the *dojo*. After meditating together, she stands opposite you and fixes you with her eyes. Using the techniques of *saiminjutsu*, she has you count down with her, "Nine, eight, seven, six . . ."

Turn to page 9.

You start down the ladder. As you descend, the voice says, "My name is Yayoi. I was on a pilgrimage with my mistress, a merchant woman from down in the valley. On the way, she broke a vase and was afraid her husband would punish her, so she pushed me into this well. Then she told everyone I'd stolen it and that I felt such remorse that I'd committed suicide by jumping in the well.

"My soul is in this mirror," Yayoi goes on as you reach the bottom of the ladder. "If you take it out of here, it will be set free. Also, you may find the mirror will help you."

You dive into the water and retrieve the mirror. Carrying it under one arm, you again make the long climb back up the well. By the time you reach the top, you're exhausted.

"So there you are!" Nada cries. "What were you doing in the well? Yukio warned us about it."

You hand Nada the mirror and collapse on the ground. "I rescued a ghost," you say when you've recovered your breath. You tell her the story, adding, "The ghost said the mirror would help us."

"I just hope you're not bewitched," Nada comments. A moment later she blurts out. "Hey, look at this!"

You sit up. Nada is looking at the mirror. In the glass you see the five ninja who attacked you, led by the one with the sword.

"They're on the road down in the valley," Nada says. "Let's go!"

Turn to page 76.

You wait for Sanchiro to leave, then you slip out. You go back to the room where the sword was, but someone has already taken it. Deciding it's too risky to look for it, you drop out the window and return safely to the woods outside the castle.

You are able to get some rest during the night, half-sleeping and half-listening for sounds of danger. Morning comes and you hide in the trees outside the castle gate, waiting for Sanchiro to appear. When he does, you hear him say something about returning as soon as he finishes off Kurayama.

You shadow Sanchiro down the path toward the village. But before he gets there, he is surprised by another ninja—who you realize must be Dana Kurayama—hiding in the trees. You can't hear what they say as they face each other, but you see them move off the path and into a clearing in the woods. Quietly you move to the edge of the clearing in time to see them kneel across from one another, bow, then stand and begin the fight. It lasts only a few minutes, during which you see an astounding series of sword moves and defensive maneuvers. Kurayama is victorious.

You rise to enter the clearing. As soon as Kurayama sees you, he disappears into the woods. Then you hear Sanchiro saying something with his last breath. You move closer. It's a curse on the Kurayama family! In a flash you realize that it is the source of the trouble at the dojo. With Nada's powers, you also know how to counteract the curse. You invoke a series of kuji signs that nullify it. Then you rush back to the village to Nada.

The End

"Finding Gyoja is probably safer," you say.

"Indeed it is," Yukio agrees.

"He's just an old monk," Gin remarks. "He won't be able to help you with ninja."

"Go back down to the village," Yukio instructs you. "Behind the biggest cedar you'll find a path. It leads up the mountain to an abandoned monastery. Gyoja occasionally sleeps there. If you do not find him you can spend the night at the monastery.

"In the morning," Yukio continues, "you can look for Gyoja higher up on the mountain."

You and Nada bow and thank the sisters for their help. As you leave, Yukio calls out, "Oh, I forgot to tell you do not go near the well at the monastery, for it is haunted. Good luck!"

Nada follows you down to the village, where you find the path behind the cedar and set off up the mountain again. The path winds through crags and dells to a flat ridge top where, at dusk, you finally reach the monastery. It is overgrown with brush and its walls are cracked and crumbling. There is no sign of Gyoja, so you and Nada eat some rice cakes and prepare to sleep.

"This place is spooky," you say.

In the morning, the monastery seems more cheerful. Walking around the building while Nada prepares breakfast, you find an old stone well. It doesn't look haunted, you think, and you're curious about what Yukio meant.

If you decide to look into the well,
turn to page 33.

If you decide you'd better not,
turn to page 109.

You close your eyes and try to relax and let your mind drift back into the dream. "I don't know. . . . I wanted you to admit you'd done some wrong. I wanted an apology or reparation."

"Some kind of compensation?"

"Sort of. . . . More like an offering. To make peace."

"Of course!" Nada says. "We should have realized it long ago. The *kami*, which was killed by my ancestor, wants a shrine."

You open your eyes. "A shrine?"

"I think Nada is right. The solution is to build a shrine," Tatsumo says. "It is the concept of *goryo shinko*. If someone, especially a warrior, dies with resentment, his spirit will seek revenge. Remember, during your trance you told us this *kami* belonged to a warrior who vowed revenge as he died at the hands of one of Nada's ancestors. Now the *kami* is back to get it. But if we build a shrine, his anger will be absorbed."

"How strange," you muse, "to build a shrine to your enemies."

"It may seem strange," Nada says, "but it happens all the time."

"Unfortunately," the *sensei* adds, "we'll have to keep you under watch until the shrine is built."

You nod in understanding. But already you feel that the venom of the *kami* is draining, and you are returning to yourself.

The End

"I just don't think we can trust Hitoshi," you insist to Nada.

"We can try to find the castle," Nada says reluctantly, "but if we're having no luck, let's get back here by dark and give Hitoshi a chance."

You and Nada return to the village and find a path up into the narrow valley Hitoshi pointed out. The path immediately splits, then splits again, and again. "We must keep careful track of these paths," Nada starts to say, "or we may never get out of—"

Suddenly something grabs your foot and whisks both of you into the air. Before you know what's happening, you are suspended between two trees by a rope around your ankle.

"Well," Nada mutters, "I guess we don't have to worry about keeping track after all."

The End

48

You look down and think to yourself that you can't imagine going back to the bottom of the well. Besides, the ghost has already tricked you once.

You continue your slow, hard climb out of the well. Yet every time you look up, the top seems no closer. Your muscles are at their limit of endurance. Vaguely, in a distant world, you hear Nada calling for you. But you have no strength left to speak. In fact, you no longer have strength enough to hold on to the ladder, and you plunge back into the water.

The End

You search the room, then move down the hall silently. Every few seconds you stop to listen. You check each of the rooms along the hallway.

In one room you make an important discovery—a scroll describing the exploits of the owner of the castle, Sanchiro Miyamotori. You try to think why the name is familiar. Then you realize it's part of the knowledge Nada gave you. Somehow you know that the Miyamotori were long-time enemies of Nada's family, the Kurayama.

You freeze as you hear footsteps in the hall. The door opens. You leap straight up twelve feet and grab on to a rafter. Two men look into the room. One of them says, "We'd better go back to the *jonin*'s chamber. He will be returning soon."

As soon as the door closes you drop soundlessly to the floor and decide to follow the two men, who you think must be Sanchiro's bodyguards. You're sure Sanchiro is the *jonin*, or head man.

You shadow the two men through the corridors of the castle. Finally they reach the entrance to Sanchiro's chamber, which is guarded by two more men. After they pass through it, you reveal yourself to the guards at the door. They move to attack you, but you hold up your hand and stop them with a look from your eyes.

You go straight to the small room on the left side of the chamber and open the sliding doors. The two men you followed, plus two more, stare at you. Before they can move, you hypnotize them with a series of *kuji* signs. You close the sliding doors, sit beside them and wait for Sanchiro to arrive.

Turn to page 36.

You settle in under the cedars to wait for Hitoshi's return. Slowly dusk comes, then twilight. You and Nada sit very still, attentive to sounds of approach.

"Listen," Nada says.

"What?"

"The insects are quiet all of a sudden—"

But her warning is too late. The attack comes from behind. You're knocked over by a blow to your head, but you react immediately by rolling out of the way of the chain your ninja attacker tries to entangle you in. You spring to your feet, assuming the defensive posture, keeping low so you can make out his shape against the stars. He feints with the chain, then aims a front kick at your head. You cut inside his kicking leg and swing your left leg out in a wide arc, catching *his* kicking leg in the air and bringing him to the ground. He jumps to his feet and disappears into the woods.

Nada is moaning on the ground a few feet away. You rush to her side. "I guess you were right about Hitoshi," she says, groaning. "He set us up. They obviously wanted to take us prisoner, or they would have killed us right away. We were lucky we could fight them off. But the one who attacked me got me with his sword. You're going to have go to on without me."

"We have to get help for you first," you insist.

Turn to page 34.

Waiting until the last two Yazuki horsemen are directly underneath, you spring from the branch.

But your timing isn't as good as Nada's. You make just enough noise as you spring that one of the samurai looks up and sees you at the last second. He knocks you away from him as you descend. You hit the ground hard. Your last thought as his sword comes down is the hope that Nada can somehow escape and finish the task on her own.

The End

You stay in the trance, giving rein to whatever force is using your body. Like a raging storm it batters everything in its path, although you can't tell how much of it is *really* happening and how much is just happening inside your head.

You soon find out. You're aware of acute bodily pain. Slowly you realize that the pain is from blows delivered by Nada and the *sensei*—and that you're returning the blows. You feel a terrible hate for the *sensei* and especially for Nada.

But now the storm seems to be passing. Your arms fall to your sides, and you slump to the floor. Your face relaxes into a mask of calmness.

Nada and the *sensei* look relieved. Tatsumo comes over to you and pounds you on the back, apparently to end the trance.

"Are you all right?" Nada asks.

"Yes," you say, motioning to Tatsumo to leave you alone. "It's all over."

"Thank goodness," Nada says. "You were in the grip of an extremely powerful *kami*, which attacked us. It was all we could do to subdue you."

"Did you find out anything?" you ask.

"Thanks to you," the *sensei* says, "we discovered it is the *kami* of a warrior who lived in the feudal era. It seems that he was an enemy of Nada's family. One of her ancestors killed him, and he vowed revenge as he died."

"I'm more convinced than ever that we must go into the past," Nada says. "But you need rest now. We can discuss our plan of action tomorrow."

You nod. A little voice inside you chuckles.

Turn to page 56.

"I'll do the trance," you say.

The *sensei* calls Tatsumo, the Shugendo priest.

Soon Tatsumo arrives. He directs that two benches be brought into the room and placed facing each other. He sits you on one, then takes the seat opposite. Nada and the *sensei* take places off to one side.

"Close your eyes," Tatsumo says, "and empty your mind. Clasp your hands in front of you. Breathe from your middle. Clear your mind as much as you can, let it go blank.

"Now," he continues, "open your eyes and look into mine. Focus on a spot directly behind my head. Do not take your eyes from mine."

Tatsumo removes a *gohei*—sacred wand—from his sleeve and places it on the bench, then begins to recite a series of prayers. As you look through his steady black eyes to the spot behind his head, you can feel yourself drifting away. Tatsumo goes into a rhythmic monotone chant, then, in a sudden spasm, ties his fingers into a knot. You recede further and further from yourself, until only a tiny bit of you is still in the *dojo*. You seem to be observing the scene from a great distance.

Tatsumo's fingers contort into knots of increasing complexity and the chant intensifies. Abruptly he stops, places the *gohei* between your clasped hands, and resumes the chant. The small part of you still dimly aware of your surroundings sees that the wand has begun to vibrate. The vibrations grow into a steady quiver. You sense another presence in the room.

Turn to page 68.

Nada leads you down a hall. "The *sensei* was very impressed with your ability to endure the trance," she says. "Here is your room. In the morning we will make some medicinal tea to help heal your bruises."

After Nada leaves, you remember the events of the past hour with greater clarity. You can see yourself attacking Nada and the *sensei*, then fighting them off as they try to pin you in the corner. All at once you realize that the moves you were making were of a different kind than the ones you've been taught. They were *ninjutsu!*

You're not sure how you know this, but it is strangely exhilarating. You feel very powerful. Your former self seems puny and insignificant.

You drift off to sleep. A dream comes to you. You're trying very hard to explain something to Nada, but you don't look like yourself. Your features are different, and you're dressed in feudal Japanese armor, with a sword at your side. Nada is similarly dressed and doesn't really look like herself either. You're trying to explain that she owes you something or must do something for you, but she doesn't seem to want to listen. You become angry. You draw your sword and swing it at her.

You awake with a feeling of hate toward Nada. You are drenched with sweat. The dream still seems real. You want to go back to sleep and find out how the dream ends. But you also wonder if you should tell Nada about your dream right now.

If you go back to sleep, turn to page 74.

If you decide to get up, turn to page 65.

You see Nada coming at you, then all goes dark.

When you open your eyes, you are immediately aware of tremendous pain throughout your body. You feel as if you've been run over by a truck. Nada, the *sensei*, and Tatsumo lean over you with looks of concern.

"I'm so sorry!" Nada says when she sees you are awake.

"You had no choice," you reply weakly. "I was attacking you."

"But I knew it wasn't really you. I knew it was the *kami*," she says.

"It's all my fault!" Tatsumo moans. "I should have seen that it had possessed you. It was very clever at hiding itself."

"It was a ninja," Nada puts in. "I realized that when we were fighting. Only a ninja would use a sword that way."

"I realized it too," you say. "I have to admit, it was thrilling to share its knowledge."

"Yes," Nada says. "It's a powerful art. But it also has great potential for evil. If you had not given up, I don't know what the outcome would have been."

"So the *kami* is defeated now?" you ask.

"Yes," she replies, "at least for the time being."

The End

You, Sashami, and Nada approach the palanquin timidly. The curtain parts, and the *daimyo* looks you over before asking Sashami his name.

After Sashami tells him, the *daimyo* says, "Aren't you the samurai who agreed to defend a village back there from the Yakuzi?"

You wonder how the *daimyo* found out about it. Sashami answers him with a weak yes and explains, "It was an impossible situation."

"Nevertheless, the code of the samurai requires you to honor you word. It is better to die in noble failure than to surrender," the *daimyo* says.

Sashami does not respond, so the *daimyo* goes on. "I will allow you to die honorably by committing *seppuku*." Your eyes widen. You know that *seppuku* is ritual suicide. "As for your attendants," the *daimyo* says, gesturing at you and Nada, "I will spare them, but they will be restricted to my castle as servants."

Not only do you feel terrible about Sashami's fate, but it looks as though it will be a while before you will be able to continue your search.

The End

The samurai hangs his head. "Many samurai are proud to die in noble failure, but not I. However, since you are both willing to stay and fight, I will join you."

"Good," Nada says briskly. "Now show us where the best spot is to lay an ambush."

The samurai, who introduces himself as Sashami, takes you to a place where the road drops into a narrow little gorge thick with trees. "This looks perfect," you say to Nada, and she agrees. You get out your gear and set up the ambush.

Moments after you've taken your positions, you hear the thunder of hooves on the road. The Yakuzi come galloping through the gorge, two abreast.

Turn to page 61.

From your perch in a tree you start the ambush by pulling a rope taut across the road, sending the horses of the first four riders to the ground.

Go on to the next page.

Sashami jumps out of the woods to take on the first two. As the second two are getting up, Nada flies from the tree opposite you, landing with a knee on the shoulder of each and knocking them to the ground.

Two more are coming on horseback. You knock one out of the saddle with a *shuriken*—a star-shaped metal throwing blade—and to the other you toss a metal ring attached to the end of long cord. He catches it easily and smiles, preparing to pull you out of the tree. But you snap the cord so that it wraps around his wrist. Then you pull him off his horse.

Just as you finish this, you see that two *more* Yakuzi are coming! You must deal with them yourself somehow, since Nada and Sashami are still occupied with the ones on the ground. You wonder if you could get the last two with a flying leap like the one Nada made. But you also remember that you have a string of firecrackers that sounds like gunfire when ignited.

If you try the leap, turn to page 52.

If you light the firecrackers, turn to page 94.

You grab the viola case and toss it to the lava globs on the shore. It quickly disappears into the molten mass.

"Thank you," the voices say. The globs appear to bow. Passing out from the heat, Nada sinks back in the lifeboat. Soon you do the same.

When you come to, the boat has drifted out of sight of the island. Nada apologizes to you. "I don't know what possessed me," she says. "For some reason I couldn't let go of the sword. I'm glad you gave it to the forge-*kami*. Now that it's back where it originated, I have a feeling our troubles are over."

"If only we can get rescued," you say.

"It won't be long," Nada tells you. "A plane flew over two hours ago. The pilot signaled that he saw us. A rescue ship is on the way."

The End

You keep yourself from going back to sleep and struggle to your feet. Your bruises throb. Your watch says it's eleven o'clock, so you are sure Nada is asleep, but you think it is important to wake her.

The feeling of anger at Nada doesn't go away—in fact, it increases. You can't control it. You hurry down the hall to Nada's room to wake her up before it completely takes over.

Nada sits up immediately when you burst into her room. You rush toward her. "Nada!" you cry with a mixture of alarm and hate. Your eyes meet hers for an instant, then with one quick motion she grabs you and pinches a nerve in your neck. You fall to the floor, unconscious.

When you come to, you are in the training hall, tied to a column. Nada, the *sensei,* and Tatsumo are there. Nada speaks your name tentatively.

"Yes," you say groggily. "What happened?"

"I'm sorry I had to do this," Nada says. "But as soon as I saw you in my room, I knew you were still possessed by the *kami.*"

You nod slowly. "Yes, I can see that now. I came to your room to tell you about a dream. In the dream, I was a feudal warrior, and so were you. I was trying to explain something, but you wouldn't listen. I got mad and drew my sword."

"What were you trying to explain?" the *sensei* asks. "Think hard. It could be important."

"I wanted Nada to do something for me. I felt that she owed me something."

"What did I owe you?" Nada prompts. "Try to remember."

Turn to page 45.

Three days later you're ready for your trip into the past. Nada explains that the energy from the sword and the *kami* will direct you to the time and place they came from. You sit in the empty *dojo* and meditate before Nada begins. She has you count down with her as she hypnotizes you with *saiminjutsu*. "Ten, nine, eight, seven . . ." The last thing you remember is Nada twisting her fingers the way Tatsumo did while putting you in the trance.

When you open your eyes you have just enough time to see you are standing beside Nada in a road near a feudal Japanese village—before being nearly run over by a samurai dressed in full battle gear. He stops, out of breath, and stares at you. His face looks earnest but frightened.

"For your own good," he says, "I suggest you get off this road and hide somewhere—anywhere."

"Why?" you ask.

"Because any minute now the Yakuzi band will come through here on horseback."

"Who are they?"

"You're lucky if you've never encountered them. They're bandit samurai who plunder towns and villages. I agreed to defend the village up the road, but that was when I thought only two or three Yakuzi were coming. Instead, I found out at least six are on the way!"

Go on to the next page.

"We'll help you defend the village," Nada says.

"Don't be ridiculous," the man replies. "You're not samurai. Even if you were, we still wouldn't have a chance."

"We have our own means," Nada says.

The samurai shakes his head. "You can escape with me if you like. I'll try to protect you. But only a fool would stay and face the Yakuzi."

Nada, however, doesn't move. It's up to you to say something.

If you say to Nada, "We should escape while we can," turn to page 28.

If you say to the samurai, "Stay and defend the village," turn to page 59.

Tatsumo stops his chanting, places his hands on your knees, and says, "Tell us, honored guest, who you are."

An unnatural male voice, not belonging to anyone in the room, but which you hazily realize is coming from your lips, says, "I am—" But the name is blocked from your hearing by a sudden crushing weight on your chest.

"What do you want?" you vaguely hear Tatsumo ask. At that moment, a wild fury is unleashed inside you. It lashes out in all directions, its enormous destructive force struggling to find something to punish. Thousands of voices scream, some for revenge, some for help. Among them you can distinguish one tiny voice, your own, but you can't hear what it is saying. You have a pressing urge to try to escape the fury inside before it destroys you.

If you try to break out of the trance, turn to page 35.

If you let it go on in order to find out what the kami wants, turn to page 53.

You follow Nada through the halls of the castle to find Mr. Hatama. On your way you run into the oldest son of the Miyamotori family. Nada bows nervously, introduces you, and says to him, "It is a pleasure to see you again, Kato."

"The pleasure is mine," Kato replies coldly. "I was under the impression you wanted to look through our archives, not nose around our castle."

"Uh, yes, you are quite right," Nada says. She has no choice but to tell him about the urn in the vault.

Kato's face turns hard with anger. "Show me this urn," he demands.

You and Nada take Kato to the dusty vault. He opens the door and turns on a light switch. The broken urn is still there—but the corpse is gone.

"This is an outrage!" Kato cries. "That urn contained the body of my uncle, who died last week. Is this how you repay the favor of letting you use our archives?"

"No, no—" Nada tries to explain.

Kato cuts her off. "You can do your explaining to the police."

You and Nada wait for the police to arrive. You will be detained while the matter is cleared up. It will be several days at least before you can get back to work on the mysterious force attacking the *dojo*—and by then it may be too late.

The End

You burst out of the side room and crouch before Sanchiro in the offensive posture. Before you can attack, something on the ground erupts into billows of smoke. You catch sight of Sanchiro jumping to a trap door in the ceiling.

You follow and find yourself in a passageway built into the ceiling. It leads to a parapet of the castle. Sanchiro is nowhere to be seen.

You think over the situation and realize that he has lured you to the place where he will have the greatest advantage. He knows every ledge of the castle top, while you are in new territory. There is one hope. You must find *ku*—the Void—and empty yourself of all preconceptions, illusions, even willpower so that you will be completely aware and ready for the attack.

It comes from the side you least expect. Sanchiro knocks you down with a crushing kidney-kite. You go limp as he comes to kick you over the edge. Your lack of resistance so surprises him that he catches his foot underneath you and pitches over the edge himself.

You get out of the castle quickly. You arrive exhausted at Nikkya's hut and tell Nada what happened.

"I'm glad you defeated Sanchiro," she says. "But I'm worried that we haven't found the exact source of the disturbances at the *dojo*. I'm also worried that we may have altered history."

"We'll have to go back right away," Nada decides. "I guess all we can do is hope that whatever you did has taken care of the problem."

The End

At breakfast you warm your hands around a bowl of rice porridge while you, Nada, and Sashami wait for the sun to come over the ridge. Sashami reminds you of his pledge to help you.

"Maybe you can help," you say. You show him the paper with the sword marking on it. "We think it may belong to a ninja clan."

Sashami's face drops when he sees the paper. "You know it?" Nada asks.

"I cannot tell you everything," Sashami replies in a low voice, "for even now it is painful to recall. I will simply say it is the secret crest of the evil Miyamotori ninja clan. It is because of the greed and deception of their leader, Sanchiro, that I was forced to leave my master, my town, and my family."

"We too have been threatened by them," Nada says.

"It would be my pleasure to help you against Sanchiro," Sashami tells you. "I can take you to the Miyamotori castle. It is two days from here if we take the Yakuzi's horses."

You ride for two days through snowy passes, grassy plains, and feudal towns until finally you reach a small village. Sashami points toward a narrow valley above the village and says, "That's where the Miyamotori castle is. I know the secret way up. Follow me carefully."

Turn to page 77.

"What are you doing?" Nada cries as you pull her out of the way of the sword and roll into the ditch on the side of the road.

Sanchiro sheaths his sword and says, "That's better. You should respect your superiors."

Angrily you get to your feet and start after him. But when he sees you coming, he simply whirls around, puts a cloak over his shoulders, and is gone.

Baffled, you look at Nada. "Cloak of invisibility," she explains. "Probably another gift from Xenglu. Why didn't you follow his instructions?"

"I was afraid it was another trick," you say sheepishly.

Nada sighs. "We blew our best chance. We may never catch up with Sanchiro now."

The End

In the middle of the night you wake up again, and, without thinking, walk out of your room and down the hall. Somehow you know where to go.

The door you want is locked. But suddenly you're on the other side of it. You find the box and open the lid. Reverently, you lift out the silk-wrapped object. You set it on the floor, unwrap it, and draw it from its sheath. Finally the sword is in your hand. It feels amazingly familiar.

You rise and go noiselessly down the hall toward the part of the *dojo* where Nada sleeps. You slip into her room and stand over her. You raise the sword. Suddenly something inside you screams, "No!" You hesitate. But in a rush your purpose returns, and you bring the sword down.

The moment of hesitation is just enough for Nada's eyes to fly open. Seeing the sword, she reacts instantaneously with a forearm deflection that blocks your sword hand. Then she hits you with a toe-strike, knocking you backward. You regain your balance and come at her. Nada flies straight up in the air to avoid the sword and catches you in the chest with a foot-stamp.

You find yourself gasping for breath on the floor. You also find that Nada's blows have weakened the *kami* inside you. You realize you've been trying to kill Nada! You see she is coming at you with a finishing blow, and you must choose between letting her deliver it, or counteracting it with one final sword move.

If you lie still, turn to page 57.

If you use the sword move, turn to page 37.

Quickly you gather your gear and light out down the mountain. In no time at all you and Nada are back in the valley, hurrying down the road to confront the ninja.

"I've been thinking," Nada says. "Yukio told us the ideogram from the sword hilt resembled the Miyamotori family crest. The Miyamotori are a ninja clan who at one time had a terrible rivalry with my family. Maybe that's who these ninja are."

You start to say it sounds likely, when suddenly, rounding a corner, you find yourself face to face with the five ninja. The leader smiles briefly, then the look of deadness you saw before comes into his eyes. He draws the sword.

"Wait!" Nada holds up her hand. "Answer one question: Are you a Miyamotori?"

"I am Sanchiro Miyamotori," he says without emotion, then advances. Just as he reaches you, you hold the mirror up to him. He freezes. Horror fills his face and the sword drops from his hand. He and the others turn and run.

After they've disappeared down the road, you turn to Nada and say, "I wonder what they saw."

"I hate to imagine," Nada replies, looking at the mirror. "It is said that a mirror can reflect your soul back to you. Whatever it was, I think we've solved our mystery and we can go back to the *dojo*."

"Should we take the sword?" you ask.

"We don't need to," Nada replies. "In the future, the sword is already at my *dojo*. Besides, it's never a good idea to tamper too much with the past."

The End

Before you reach the castle, you hear a yell from the woods. Cautiously the three of you dismount and investigate.

You come upon a clearing in which two ninja are faced off against each other. Each has a sword. They kneel and bow, then slowly approach one another.

"That's Sanchiro Miyamotori!" Sashami whispers.

"And he's got the sword—the one that's at the *dojo* now!" you add.

You grab Sashami's sword from him, ready to rush out and help the other ninja. But then you wonder if it's a good idea. Maybe you should let the two ninja fight it out themselves.

If you go ahead into the clearing,
turn to page 112.

If you stay back, turn to page 107.

"Let's try to find out where the sword came from," you say.

"I'll bring it in," Nada says. "We can take a closer look at it."

The sword is wrapped in silk. Nada places it on the table, unrolls the silk, and pulls the sword out of its scabbard. Its blade is sharper than anything you've ever seen. But it's the markings on the hilt that draw your attention.

"This is an odd symbol," the *sensei* says. "I don't know what it stands for. Some kind of secret sect, perhaps."

"It almost looks like a family crest," you say.

"Yes," the *sensei* says. "In fact, it reminds me a little of the Miyamotori family crest."

"The Miyamotori!" Nada exclaims. "They were once the sworn enemies of my family."

"Are they still?" you ask.

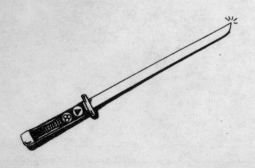

Go on to the next page.

"Not really," Nada replies, "but these rivalries die very slowly. We'd better track down the person who sent us the sword and find out where they got it."

"That may be difficult," the *sensei* says. "There was little information enclosed with the sword. What about doing some research into the history of the Miyamotori family? You may find something that tells you about the ideogram on the hilt."

"But that would mean asking the Miyamotori family to let us look at their archives," Nada says.

"Luckily I have a good friend who is a *sensei* at their *ryu*. We could call him to help arrange your visit," the *sensei* says.

Nada turns to you and asks, "What do you think?"

If you say, "Let's do some research,"
turn to page 87.

If you say, "Let's try to find the person who sent the sword," turn to page 101.

You and Nada carefully circle the corpse. While Nada waits on one side, you stand across from her and reach down to look at the body.

When you turn the corpse over a horrible demon mask stares back up at you. Suddenly the white eyes come alive. They grip you as if binding you with rope. The rope squeezes tighter and tighter. Nada frantically attacks the demon-corpse, but her blows bounce off it as if it were made of steel. You struggle to maintain consciousness. Nada, desperate enough to try anything, pulls the demon mask off the face of the corpse. The grip on you loosens, and Nada immediately ties her fingers into a series of strange knots. It's over in a matter of moments—the corpse once again lifeless, this time for real.

"What happened?" you ask, still dazed. "When you pulled off the mask, it seemed to lose its power."

"I don't think the mask had any real power. Pulling it off just distracted him and gave me an opening," Nada explains. "I think the corpse was possessed by a ninja *kami,* the *kami* that has been attacking our *dojo.* I was able to use *kuji*—a form of sorcery I learned in my ninja training—to scare it away. It may return, though."

"At least it won't be back for a little while," you say. "Maybe in the meantime we can figure out where it came from and what it wants."

The End

You shake off your premonition and vow not to be so jumpy. A second later flames burst all around you. Every way you turn, you see fire. Nada pulls you out of the road, but already a net has landed over your head. You're trapped. Five figures clad in black ninja clothes emerge from the woods and move in on you.

You have no idea why, but you are about to be the target of a ninja assassination.

The End

"We've got to get rid of the sword," you say to Nada. "It's obviously the source of our trouble."

"We can't do that," Nada objects. "How can we track down who sent it?"

"We'll copy the markings on the hilt. That's all we need."

"I don't know. . . ." Nada says.

The stewardess decides for you. She grabs the sword and tosses it overboard. Nada reaches for it as it sails over the railing, but she can't catch it. The sword sinks into the sea.

Soon the captain of the freighter comes on again to announce, "The engines seem to be fixed, folks. We'll have you back on land soon."

The freighter takes you to Wake Island. Nada immediately calls the *sensei* to tell him what happened. The *sensei* takes the news calmly, remarking only that the air at the *dojo* seems lighter.

You and Nada return to the *dojo*. You stay for a few more days. No lightning storms or other strange events recur. One day as you and Nada sip tea with the *sensei*, he announces, "I think we can consider our mystery solved. The disturbances have ceased. The sword obviously brought with it some sort of angry spirit, and now it and the spirit's anger are at the bottom of the sea."

You and Nada agree. You prepare to catch a train back to Kyoto the next day, glad to have had the visit with Nada.

The End

The crew of the freighter lowers a lifeboat into the water, followed by you, Nada, and the viola case. They include water and a week's supply of space-food sticks, and wish you luck.

Once you've left the ship, its engines apparently recover and it steams away at rapid speed. You find yourselves alone in the middle of the Pacific.

Two days later you are still there. The sword is quiet, and you haven't seen a single ship or plane. "We must be out of the shipping lanes," you say.

Later in the day you spot a pillar of smoke on the horizon. "Look!" you cry. "Maybe it's a ship."

But as the smoke grows into a black cloud and fire shoots into the sky, you realize it's no ship. You watch in awe as the eruption builds. Great columns of flame burst forth.

A cone-shaped piece of land rises from the sea. Your boat drifts toward the new island. The heat is intense as you float to the shore. Nada begins to row away from the hot land.

"Wait!" you say. "Something's on the shore."

Globs of lava rise out of the molten rock, seeming to stand up to greet you. They don't appear to have mouths, but you hear a deep, raspy voice say, "We are the gods of the forge and swordmaking. You have a sword that is causing disruption in our world. You must give it to us."

Nada is defiant. "Never!"

If you don't want to give it to them either, turn to page 106.

If you think you should throw the sword to the lava creatures, turn to page 63.

"Luckily I have seen enough of this type of thing that I may be able to keep my reputation as a wise man intact," Gyoja says with a little smile. "I believe you are dealing with an angry *kami*. Almost certainly it is the *kami* of the ninja who ambushed you. I suspect the arrival of his sword at your *dojo* aroused the anger of the *kami*. I can't say why he was angry in the first place, but what is important is to placate it."

"But it's attacking us," you object.

"Most attacks are best fended off with understanding," Gyoja replies. "Violence breeds more violence."

"How can we make peace with the *kami*?" Nada asks.

"Build a shrine to it," Gyoja says. "Use the sword in the shrine. Have a summer festival for it. If you do this with sincerity, the anger of the *kami* will be absorbed by the greater *kami*."

You and Nada bow deeply and thank Gyoja for sharing his advice. Then you head down to the monastery to spend the night. In the morning you will return to the present and try out Gyoja's suggestion.

The End

The next day you and Nada take the train to the remote village below the Miyamotori estate. A taxi leaves you at the estate, a forbidding castle set back in a dark valley.

After a long climb up stone steps and through several gates, you ring the bell. The *rojo*—house mistress—answers. Acknowledging that Mr. Hatama arranged for your visit, she leads you to the cramped archive room in a remote part of the castle.

After the *rojo* leaves, Nada remembers that she promised the *sensei* she'd give his regards to Mr. Hatama. "I'll be back in a few minutes," she tells you.

You start searching through the thick, tattered parchments while Nada is gone. Only a minute later you hear a loud rattling noise. It seems to be coming from down the hall. At first you ignore it, but it becomes so loud and insistent you can't concentrate on the papers.

Cautiously you walk down the hall to a heavy, squat door. You check to see that no one is watching, and try the door. It opens.

Turn to page 99.

"I would like you to give me your sword," the Sea Queen says. "I know it's a big request. It is not easy to give up such a powerful weapon."

"But we do not intend to use it," Nada protests.

"You are entitled to an explanation," the Queen goes on. "The sword belonged to a ninja warrior of the feudal period. His name was Sanchiro Miyamotori. Much of his power came from his sword, which was given to him by a *tengu*. The *tengu* also taught him magic."

Nada whispers to you that a *tengu* is a beaked, winged creature that lives in trees in the mountains.

"Unfortunately," the Sea Queen continues, "Sanchiro misused what the *tengu* taught him. He caused so much trouble that he was confronted by another ninja, Dana Kurayama" (Nada whispers to you that he was her ancestor), "who killed Sanchiro. As Sanchiro was dying, he vowed revenge on the Kurayama. When your *dojo* received the sword it inflamed the ninja's vengeful *kami*, and his vow was set in motion."

"How can we counteract it?" you ask.

"Give me the sword," the Sea Queen answers. "The *kami*'s anger will drain away."

Nada hands the sword to the Sea Queen. The Queen thanks her. Nada bows low and responds, "We should thank you for solving our problem, and for allowing us to be guests in your palace."

The Queen waves her hand. "Just do not tell anyone you have seen me."

You and Nada turn and are led from the palace, wondering if the *sensei* will believe your story.

The End

"Just a quick look," Nada says.

You take Nada down the hall, pause at the door, then step inside. The door swings closed behind you. It is pitch dark in the room, and the air is heavy.

"I can feel it in here—the presence of the *kami!*" Nada whispers.

You light a match. The broken shards of the urn are still on the floor, but the corpse is gone!

You hear a scraping sound at the other end of the vault. You and Nada creep toward it, the match illuminating a tiny space in front of you. Finally, you reach the back wall. You can see nothing else, just three stone walls.

"This is not an ordinary wall," Nada says, her hands feeling the stone. She directs the match to a crack in the corner. "It's a secret doorway." She pushes it, and part of the wall swivels open.

"How could you tell?" you ask.

Nada stops for a moment. "There's something I've never told you which I guess you'd better know now," she says. "Before I began aikido, I had another kind of training—*ninjutsu.* My family has been a ninja clan for many centuries. So have the Miyamotori."

Go on to the next page.

She pauses while you absorb this revelation. Ninja were supposed to have amazing powers, not only in the martial arts, but in techniques of invisible movement and even sorcery.

"So we may be dealing with a ninja?" you say.

"Possibly," Nada says. "It's still hard to tell what this is all about."

"Maybe we should go back to the archives," you suggest. "We may find something in our research that will help us figure this out before we fall into some kind of trap."

"Yes," Nada replies, "except that if we're on its trail, I'd hate to lose it."

If you push for going back to the archives, turn to page 102.

If you decide it's a good idea to go into the secret passage, turn to page 22.

On the plane, you stash the sword safely in the overhead luggage compartment. The plane taxis down the runway and soon you are on your way to San Francisco. But you are not in the air long before a passenger walking past your seat trips and falls for no apparent reason. Then a stewardess suddenly upends a tray full of breakfast all over your lap, causing you to jump around as hot tea soaks through your clothes.

Things seem to calm down after breakfast, but then a ruckus starts in the overhead compartment. You open the door. The viola case is bouncing furiously against the walls inside. The pilot comes over the speaker and says, "Ladies and gentlemen, I'm sorry to report that our engines are failing. We're going to make a crash landing in the ocean. Please fasten your seat belts. I've radioed for help."

The stewardesses move about the cabin quickly, making preparations and calming the screaming passengers. The plane plunges. Miraculously, no one is hurt in the crash landing. Rafts are inflated, emergency doors are opened, and the occupants of the plane are evacuated. In the confusion, Nada grabs the sword.

Turn to page 97.

You toss the firecrackers in front of the last two Yakuzi. They go off in sequence, sending staccato reports through the gorge.

The effect is better than you hoped for. The horses rear and turn, and the other Yakuzi panic at the sound. "We're surrounded!" one cries. They turn and flee, following the two on horseback. Nada and Sashami allow them to escape, making sure their horses stay behind.

You climb out of the tree, and Nada congratulates you on the firecracker tactic. "It was a brilliant application of the technique of illusion," she says. "When hopelessly outnumbered, create the illusion of having greater numbers."

Sashami bows to both of you. "Had I known I had such skilled ninja as allies, I would not have hesitated to confront the Yakuzi."

"Do you think they'll come back?" you ask.

"Oh no," Sashami assures you. "They won't return after the treatment we gave them."

Sashami goes on to explain he is a *ronin*—a kind of freelance samurai who has no master and travels about looking for what work he can find. "With your help, I've fulfilled my obligation to the village. Now I will fulfill my obligation to you. I am at your service."

"We're all tired from the fight. Let's make camp and discuss this in the morning," Nada says.

Turn to page 72.

You move slowly into the middle of the circle, hoping your improvised dance doesn't look too funny to the *yamabushi*. But then you get an idea. You act out your dilemma for them. Half-singing, half-talking as you dance, you tell of your search for the ninja, the meeting with the Mikiaka sisters, and Nada's abduction by the *tengu*. As the song comes to an end, you pose the question, "Can anyone tell me how to rescue my friend?"

The *yamabushi* clap and cheer appreciatively after your performance. Anxiously you look for the one who invited you in. "What about my question?" you cry when you find him.

"Few can outwit the *tengu*," he answers simply. "You'll just have to hope he takes pity on you."

He pulls you back into the circle, and reluctantly you join the merriment while you try to figure out what to do. But somehow as you dance you forget your troubles. You are given several gifts, including a string of pearls and a dragon's head hat. You don't remember falling asleep.

You awake alone in the clearing beside the smoldering ashes of the fire. Everything is gone. The pearls are drops of water and the dragon's head a mere trinket.

You get to your feet shakily. Suddenly a strong wind comes up. It swirls into a whirlwind that lifts you off the ground and carries you to the top of the mountain, depositing you at the foot of a cryptomeria tree. You hear laughter from the branches of the tree above you. You look up—and see Nada and the *tengu* flying down to join you.

Turn to page 26.

"What's our strategy when we get to the top of the ladder?" you ask Nada.

"It will require you to go to the limit of your defensive skill," Nada says. "You climb the ladder first. I'll be a few feet behind you. You must be ready for anything at the top. If you can hold it off for just a few seconds, that will give me my chance to grab it. Be prepared—it will probably be extremely vicious."

You nod, take a moment to prepare yourself, and begin climbing the ladder. You reach the top and carefully you feel what is above you.

"It's a trap door," you whisper to Nada.

"Okay," she whispers back. "Open it . . . now!"

You push open the door and immediately swing away from it, one hand still holding the ladder. Something—it feels like the jaws of an animal—grabs your arm. You see Nada catapult straight up past you as if shot out of a cannon. A second later there is a bright flash, then puffs of smoke.

"Come on up," Nada says, coughing in the smoke. "He used a smoke bomb to get away."

You untangle the thing around your arm—it's a *kusari-fundo*, a chain with metal weights on each end—and climb through the trap door. As the smoke clears, you find you're on a parapet. Below are the ramparts, walls, and courtyards of the castle. There is no sign of your attacker.

"I have no doubt now that we are dealing with a ninja," Nada says. "Why he's attacking us, I don't know. But he managed to escape our counter-trap. Now we need a new strategy."

Turn to page 104.

A few hours later a freighter arrives to pick you up. Once on board, some passengers laugh and some cry in relief. But after a few minutes a high piercing note comes from inside the viola case. The captain of the freighter announces, "I hate to say this folks, but our engines are malfunctioning. Stand by while we locate the trouble."

Everyone glares at you. The stewardess who spilled the tray comes over and says, "Look here, I don't know what you've got in that viola case, but I've got a feeling it's causing all this. Either it goes or you do."

"No!" Nada cries. "We can't give up this case. We have to find out what's going on!"

If you think you should try to convince Nada to throw the sword overboard, turn to page 83.

If you agree that you must hold on to it, turn to page 84.

It takes a moment for your eyes to adjust to the dim green light. When they do, you see you are in a large, dusty vault. Suits of armor hang from the walls, some of them containing skeletons. But it is the big urn in the center of the room that causes the rattling as it spins madly on its base. Greenish lights hover above it. It spins faster and faster until it topples to the ground, smashing into pieces and revealing what is inside—a corpse, whose dead white eyes stare at you!

Hastily you back out of the room, close the door, and return to the archives. When Nada returns you tell her, as calmly and precisely as you can, what you just saw.

"This is very bad," she says. "We must avoid trouble here. We're not welcome guests. We'd better tell Mr. Hatama."

If you say, "Don't you want to look for yourself first?," turn to page 90.

If you agree that Mr. Hatama should be consulted, turn to page 69.

.

"Let's look for another way around," you say. "I don't like the idea of walking into a trap, even if we are prepared for it."

"It would be foolish to climb the ladder if you have doubts," Nada agrees.

You and Nada go back to the intersection of passageways and take a right. The passage twists and curves, seeming to go nowhere.

"I've lost track of where we are," you say.

"It was built to do that," Nada replies. "We must be careful when we finally find a way out of it. The ninja, or whatever it is, may know exactly where we are going to emerge."

At last you do come to a dead end in the passage. Nada feels around for the secret door. "We have to be ready for anything," she whispers. "Flatten yourself against the wall on the other side of the door. When I open it, I'll jump back on this side, and we'll see if anything is waiting for us."

You cross to the wall on the other side. Nada swings the door open quickly, then jumps away from it. Light pours in through the opening.

You wait for five, ten, fifteen minutes. Nothing happens. You don't hear a sound. Carefully you and Nada move to the door and through it to a stone courtyard. Lying face down in the middle of the courtyard is the corpse.

If you decide to look at the corpse, turn to page 81.

If you think you should tell Nada it's time to talk to Mr. Hatama about the bizarre events, turn to page 115.

You and Nada find the letter that came with the sword. There is no return address and no signature.

"I don't know how we can track down the sender," Nada says.

"Can we find the box it came in?"

After you manage to dig up the box the sword came in, you check the wrapping paper for a postmark.

San Francisco!" you exclaim.

"Then I guess that's where we're going," Nada says. "We can catch a plane from Kyoto in the morning."

You and Nada wrap the sword and put it in a viola case to take on the plane to California. You get your ticket at the airport and head to the boarding gate. As you approach the metal detector you realize you will have to pass through it with the sword.

"What are we going to do?" Nada whispers as you wait in line. "They'll never let us take the sword on the plane."

"It's too late to go back," you say in a low voice. "We can say it's an heirloom."

"This better work," Nada replies.

You go through the detector first. Nada places the viola case on the conveyor belt. No sirens, bells, or buzzers sound. Nada picks it up and you walk to the gate. "I hope there are no hijackers trying to get on this flight," she murmurs.

"Maybe this is just a very weird sword," you reply.

Turn to page 92.

"Let's go back to the archives," you say. "I've got a hunch we may turn up something there."

You go back through the vault and return to your research. Finally your tired eye catches it— the ideogram on the sword.

"Here it is!" you say to Nada. You discover the ideogram was the secret crest of a ninja *ryu* founded four hundred years ago by Sanchiro Miyamotori. According to legend, Sanchiro was taught the art of *ninjutsu,* as well as sorcery, by a *tengu*—a mythical long-nosed, winged creature supposed to live in trees in the mountains. The *tengu* gave Sanchiro a sword, which was the source of his powers.

Sanchiro exercised his power to accumulate a large amount of land and wealth. But one day he was cut down by another ninja named Dana Kurayama—an ancestor of Nada's. Sanchiro died cursing the Kurayama clan and vowing revenge.

"That's the answer!" Nada cries. "The force disturbing our *dojo* is the *kami* of Sanchiro Miyamotori. When we received his sword, it inflamed the desire for revenge. Whoever sent us the sword wanted to stir up trouble between our families. I'm sure that what was in the vault was the *kami* in another form, trying to lure us into a trap."

"Then maybe if we return the sword to the Miyamotori—" you begin.

"Yes!" Nada exclaims. "Good idea. I'm sure they'd be pleased to get it back. Not only will it calm the *kami,* but it could be the beginning of a reconciliation between our families."

The End

You pull a *shuriken* from your *furoshiki* and let it fly at the *tengu*. It hits his wing, causing him to howl in surprise. He glares at you with flashing eyes, and shrieks, "How dare you!"

The *tengu* lets go of Nada and rises into the air, his injured wing flapping weakly. Your rush on to the bridge to help Nada. The *tengu* laughs. Suddenly the bridge bursts into flame. It is quickly consumed in the fire, and you and Nada plunge into the ravine.

The End

"Why don't we split up?" you suggest. "That way we have a better chance of finding him, and he can't attack us both at once."

"All right," Nada agrees. "But be careful. Try to be attuned to *sakki,* to the force of the killer. Let's meet here in twenty minutes if we find no clues."

You nod, and the two of you split up to look for the ninja. You climb down the parapet and go along one of the stone ramparts, moving with *ha-ragei.* You follow the rampart to an outer running wall, from which you can survey the tiled roofs and curved gables of the castle. On the other side of the wall is a long, sheer drop into a ravine.

Suddenly you roll to the left, dropping off the wall and hanging on to the top of it by your hands. A black-clad figure lands for a second at the spot you just left, but his momentum—which he expected you to break—carries him off the wall and into the ravine below. As he goes by, you see his eyes are the white eyes of the corpse.

You pull yourself back up on the wall and call to Nada. You tell her what happened. "I don't know how I knew he was coming," you say. "I didn't think about it. I just got out of the way."

"That's *sakki,*" Nada says.

"What about the corpse?" you wonder. "How could it attack me?"

"I think the *kami* must have possessed the body of the dead man in order to attack us. But I still don't know why the ninja wanted to kill us."

"We'd better get out of here," you say. "I'll bet the *sensei* will have some ideas."

The End

You try to explain to the lava creatures that you must keep the sword to find out what force is attacking Nada's *dojo*. Meanwhile, Nada begins to row away from the shore.

"Come back!" the voices cry. "You must give us the sword. It will only cause more disruption!"

The voices fade as you pull away from the island. You catch a current that takes you out to the open sea again. But you don't feel as if you're drifting. Something seems to be pulling you, and it is getting stronger. The boat moves faster and faster toward the source of the current.

Finally you catch a glimpse of what is drawing you—a huge whirlpool in the sea! You try to row away from it, but you are firmly in its grip. You feel as if you're going over a waterfall as you're sucked over the edge of the gigantic whirlpool. Into the maelstrom you rush, spinning down, down, down. You cover your head in a fruitless gesture as the great weight of the water closes over you.

When you open your eyes you and Nada are amazed to find yourselves in an underwater palace festooned with seaweed. Three white-scaled dragon-women are pulling your boat through the grand phosphorescent corridors of the palace.

You are led to a throne, where a woman wearing a crown with a serpent on it is sitting on a cushion playing the *biwa*, a stringed instrument. The woman looks up and greets you, saying, "You are probably wondering where you are. Do not be afraid. I am the Sea Queen, and this is my palace."

"Did you bring us down here?" you ask.

"Yes," the Sea Queen replies. "I have something important to ask of you."

Turn to page 89.

Nada grabs you at the same moment that you decide to stay back. "We can't meddle," she says. "The other ninja will do better without us."

"I just realized that," you reply

The battle between the two ninja begins. You can barely follow the quick succession of sword moves, parries, and jumps before the other ninja cuts down Sanchiro.

Sashami leaps out to congratulate the ninja, but when the ninja sees him, he runs into the woods. You and Nada creep into the clearing.

"Listen!" you say. "Sanchiro's saying something."

You hear Sanchiro's dying words: a curse of revenge on the Kurayama family—Nada's family!

"The other ninja must have been my ancestor," Nada says. "We've witnessed the origin of the *kami*'s vow of revenge. When our *dojo* got the sword, it must have set the vow into action."

"Can we counteract it?" you ask.

"We can try," Nada says. She goes through a series of finger signs similar to the ones you saw when she brought you into the past with her. When she is finished, she turns to you and says, "Even if my *kuji* doesn't work, now that we know the origin of the curse, I think we'll be able to offset it with the *sensei*'s help."

Meanwhile, Sashami returns and says sheepishly, "I guess I scared away the ninja."

"No matter," you say. "Without your help, we never could have solved our problem."

You say good-bye to Sashami and prepare to return to the *dojo*.

The End

Leaving the sword for later, you spring for the ninja, who appears to be having trouble getting up. But suddenly he turns and flings something in your face that causes your eyes to burn. At the same time, you hear Nada attack the other two. The ninja disappears, but a few seconds later you are thrown on your back from behind, and the sword is put to your abdomen.

"Stop!" the ninja cries to Nada. "I've got your friend!"

You and Nada are tied up and taken back to the ninja's castle. Because your adversary knows all the methods of escape, there is no chance for you and Nada to get away. After a few days in the dungeon, you are brought before the ninja in his chamber. You are made to kneel at the foot of the platform on which he sits.

"To be frank," he says, "you surprised us. We were lying in wait for someone else. We still can't figure out where you came from, but it is obvious you are skilled ninja. Perhaps fate wanted us to meet."

"What do you mean?" you ask.

"We want you to join us. It is a great opportunity for you. I have learned many powers from a *tengu* in the mountains, and with the sword he gave me I am invincible. Already, as you can see, we have accumulated much land and wealth. We will accumulate more."

"And if we don't want to join you?" Nada asks.

The ninja shrugs. "Then you will die."

The End

Deciding it's better to stay away from the haunted well, you return to have breakfast with Nada. After you eat, you set off up the mountain to find Gyoja.

You search all day, but can find no sign of the *yamabushi*. You are about to give up when you catch sight of a small shrine hidden in the trees. There you find a tiny, withered old man with long hair and a conch trumpet at his side. He looks startled when you approach him.

"Even here you find me!" he exclaims. "I've been avoiding you all day, trying to do my work. Whatever you want, it must be important."

"It is," Nada says, bowing. She relates the details of the situation at the *dojo*, as well as the attack by the ninja and his sword.

"Yukio thought you might be able to help us," Nada concludes.

Turn to page 86.

You ignore the *koto* music and continue up the mountain, your eyes fixed on the *tengu-bi*. The lights seem to grow brighter and brighter as you climb through the night.

When you reach the ridge just below the *tengu-bi*, the lights suddenly burst into a web of lightning bolts. They flash madly, covering the sky above you, illuminating the landscape. Thunder cracks and booms. A wild, whirling wind whips the trees into frenzied motion.

You look for some place to take cover, but the wind and lightning seem to penetrate everything. Then out of the sky swoops the *tengu*, his eyes blazing, sparks flying from his wings, claws poised. You turn and run down the mountain. The *tengu* flies after you, swooping in on your head, then pulling away at the last second, over and over again. Finally he cries, "I thought you could do better than this!"

He pulls away, and a wind funnel of sticks and rocks picks you up off the mountain, carries you out across the range, across the Sea of Japan, and deposits you in a tiny village below the Great Wall of China.

The End

"No!" Nada whispers sharply as you rush forward with Sashami's sword. She tries to grab you, but misses. This distracts the other ninja, and in a flash Sanchiro strikes. The ninja falls.

Then Sanchiro turns to face you. You come at him—and with your first strike, your sword breaks in two on his. You realize you've made a terrible mistake. Sanchiro's sword has some kind of magical power, and there is no way you'll be able to defend yourself against it.

The End

You grab the sword and slip back out the window. You climb over the castle wall and return undetected to Nikkya's house.

You knock on the door. Nikkya answers and motions for you to keep quiet. "I think Nada will pull through," she whispers, "but she must sleep. You can talk to her in the morning."

Although you're impatient to show Nada the sword, you realize the old woman is right. Exhausted yourself, you soon fall asleep.

In the morning you find Nada weak but otherwise recovering well. You tell her of your exploits and show her the sword. But her reaction is not what you expect.

"I'm very impressed that you were able to get the sword," she says, "but I'm not sure how it will help us. After all, we already have it—in our time—at the *dojo*. What we really need to find out is the source of the disturbance. We still don't know that."

"You're right," you say. "I didn't think of it that way."

"Well, Nikkya had some helpful information. After she fixed up my wound, she told me that the castle belongs to Sanchiro Miyamotori. The Miyamotori were enemies of my family for a long time. That may help us figure out what is going on. All we can do now is return to our time and hope the *sensei* can help us put things together."

The End

"No thanks," you say to the *yamabushi*. "I have to rescue my friend."

Quickly you slip back into the woods and head for the road. But you can't seem to find it. You keep searching in the dark, until you realize you're going in circles. Exhausted and bleeding from fighting through the thicket, you finally collapse in sleep.

You wake up the next morning and decide to forget about the road and to hike straight up the mountain. All morning you bushwack through the dense wood. Finally you come to a clearing on top of a ridge.

What you see causes you to draw in your breath sharply. There is nothing but water all around you. You are on top of an island, a lone mountain sitting in the middle of the blue ocean. You have a feeling some kind of sorcery brought you here—maybe the *yamabushi* taking revenge for your refusal to join them—but you have no idea how you're going to get back to civilization.

The End

"This is getting very strange," you say to Nada. "I think we'd better tell Mr. Hatama about it."

"I suppose you're right," Nada replies. "If the Miyamotori family catches us here with this corpse, we'll be in a lot of trouble."

You and Nada begin to walk out of the courtyard to look for Mr. Hatama. A slight sound makes you look behind you. You turn just in time to see the corpse, wearing a horrible demon mask, bringing a sword down at your neck.

The End

ABOUT THE AUTHOR

JAY LEIBOLD was born in Denver, Colorado. He has also written *Sabotage, Grand Canyon Odyssey, Spy for George Washington, The Antimatter Formula,* and *Beyond the Great Wall* for the Choose Your Own Adventure series.

ABOUT THE ILLUSTRATOR

S. FREYMANN lives in New York City, where he makes paintings and drawings in a little apartment filled with books and musical instruments.

New 5/91